# Contents

Series Reading Consultant: Prue Goodwin
Reading and Language Information Centre,
University of Reading

# Chapter One

Boris the mouse was waiting on the north-bound platform at Camden Town station. He lived underground in the London tube. That's the railway that takes people backwards and forwards underneath the big city. It was a quiet afternoon.

The only noise came from a
small office at one end of the
platform.

"Hurrah!" Boris heard, and then someone shouted, "That ref must be mad!" It was Boris's friend Heavy Duty.

Heavy Duty was a human who worked as a cleaner at the station. He liked Boris and sometimes let him ride on the broom while he swept the platform.

In the afternoons Heavy Duty would sit in his little office and watch football on the television. Boris's cousin Kicker often watched it too.

Man and mouse were both football mad. In fact Boris was nearly knocked over when Kicker came charging out of the cupboard.

"On the head! On the head!" cried Kicker. He loved football even more than cheese – which is saying a lot for a mouse. Kicker had a squashed-up piece of chewing-gum paper, which he was bouncing on his head like a football. "Wembley!" he shouted, allowing the ball to drop down onto one of his tiny feet. "See that, Boris? I'm getting really good.

I could play in the World Cup,
you know. You should have seen
the match. It was faaaantastic!
On the head! On the head!"
Kicker bounced about as he
spoke. He was a very confident
little mouse.

Heavy Duty came out
onto the platform to get
on with his work. He
grabbed his wide
broom and started
sweeping.

One of the station's regular passengers arrived to wait for a train. It was old Mrs Brett. She didn't see Boris and Kicker. That wasn't surprising – most people didn't notice the tube mice. But Kicker noticed *her*. She was carrying a shopping bag and a brand new, black and white, real leather football.

Mrs Brett stopped by Heavy
Duty. "Good morning," she said
brightly. She was a friendly
woman.

"Morning, Mrs Brett," said Heavy Duty, smiling. He nodded at the football. "You playing for England, then?" he joked.

Mrs Brett laughed. "It's for my granddaughter." She held up the shiny new ball. "It's her birthday. She's football mad." Then the old woman bent down and put the football in her shopping bag.

"Look!" whispered Kicker in awe. "A *real* football! I'd give anything to have a go."

"You're too little," said Boris. "That football is huge."

But Kicker wasn't listening.
He ran full speed along the
platform towards Mrs Brett as if
he was about to score a goal. He
was tired of playing football
with bits of old paper. He
wanted to get a close look at a
real ball.

Just then the next train came roaring towards the platform from the dark tunnel entrance. It caused a bit of a draught. Boris had to hang onto one of Heavy Duty's shoelaces to stop himself being blown away.

Mrs Brett staggered slightly
and knocked over her shopping
bag.

The ball fell out
and bounced. It
bounced
just as the doors to
the train opened.

The football bounced twice
more on the platform and then
shot into the train. It bounced
onto the floor, past someone's
feet and away down the
crowded carriage.

"Hey, your ball!" shouted
Kicker – but of course Mrs Brett
didn't hear. People waiting for
trains don't expect mice to call
out to them. Usually they don't
even notice they are there.

Mrs Brett did nothing. She didn't realize what had happened. This was not the train she wanted so she just stood waiting on the platform.

The guard waved from the end of the train. He was ready to shut the doors again. Kicker squared his shoulders, ready to make the save of the day. With a cry of, "Don't worry, I'll get it," he did something tube mice should never do. He jumped onto the train.

Boris let go of Heavy Duty's shoelace immediately. "Kicker!" he shouted. "Come back."

But Kicker was inside the train chasing the ball. Boris knew this was a disaster. The train might take him anywhere.

With a sigh Boris summoned up
all his courage and jumped into
the carriage. The doors closed
behind him.

# Chapter Two

The train set off with a jolt and
the football bounced against
someone's shoe. It was a
businessman reading the paper.

He didn't look down but when
he crossed his legs he
accidentally flicked the ball to
the other side of the carriage.

The train was very full and the passengers were all busy reading their books and newspapers. No-one paid any attention to the football. It was jostled from one foot to another.

Kicker was determined to reach it. Each time it bounced away down the carriage he ran after it and Boris chased after him.

By the next stop Kicker was right up at the other end of the carriage. He was just about to grab the ball when the train stopped rather suddenly. Boris had nothing to hold onto.

He flew through the air and landed in a great heap on top of a rather surprised Kicker.

The doors opened and the ball rolled out onto the platform. It bounced twice and landed in the lap of a toddler sitting in a buggy. The toddler's mother was much too busy trying to balance all her shopping to notice.

"Boris!" Kicker shouted crossly. "I nearly had the ball just then."

"Well, it's gone now," said Boris, getting up and brushing himself down. "It's bounced off the train and we're in big trouble because . . ." But before Boris could finish his sentence, his cousin was off again.

"Quick!" shouted Kicker. He jumped off the train and ran towards the buggy. Boris had no choice but to follow him.

There was a large net bag
hanging down from the handles
of the pushchair. Kicker grabbed
one end and hauled himself up
just as the woman started off
towards the exit.

"Kicker!" yelled Boris, running along beside the buggy – but Kicker was climbing up the bag towards the ball. It was only at the last moment that Boris managed to grab the end of the net bag and haul himself up.

The baby's mother pushed the buggy along to the end of the platform and a man stopped to help her up the escalator. Soon the baby, the ball and the two mice were heading for the park.

Boris had got his foot caught in the net bag. "Help me," he whispered urgently, but Kicker was busy. The large toddler sitting in the buggy had picked him up by the tail.

"Help, it's going to eat me!" shrieked Kicker.

"Don't be silly," said Boris,
trying to pull his foot free.
"Babies don't eat mice."

But the baby didn't seem to
know this. It held Kicker up and
opened its mouth . . .

## Chapter Three

Suddenly the mother spotted
Kicker in her child's sticky little
fist. "Aaagh!" she shrieked. She
grabbed Kicker from the baby
and threw the poor mouse into
the air.

Kicker flew in a great arc, finally landing on the lap of a large lady who was sitting on a bench reading a book.

She was eating a family-size packet of cheese and onion crisps and didn't seem to notice.

At last Boris pulled his foot free and scrambled off the buggy to the ground. He would have been fine if the baby's mother hadn't been quite so upset.

"Go away!" she shouted. She picked up the football and threw it at Boris. It landed on his head and bounced into a flower bed.

"Ow!" cried Boris and rubbed his head. He felt dizzy. He wanted to sit down but there wasn't time. "Kicker! Kicker! Are you all right?" he called up to the large lady's lap.

"Mmm . . . fine . . . mm," came the reply.

"This is no time to eat!" shouted Boris.

"I have had a very difficult day," replied Kicker, stuffing bits of crisp into his mouth.

"We've got to—" But Boris didn't finish his sentence because suddenly he saw a man in black shorts and a striped shirt pick up the football from the flower bed.

"Here we are – here's the ball," said the man and gave it to a small girl.

He blew his whistle. "Let's play!" he cried.

"Oh no!" yelled Boris, watching as the football disappeared into a crowd of children in games kit. He just knew Kicker wouldn't be able to leave it alone.

To a small mouse like Kicker the football pitch looked like Wembley. He had seen football matches on Heavy Duty's television but of course he had never been to a real game. He scrambled down from the bench, pushed past Boris and rushed along the touchline. "On the

head! On the head!" he shouted, but no-one could hear him.

Boris was beside himself. They were probably miles from home, he had a bad headache and he was about to see his cousin squashed by a troop of studded boots. It would be very difficult to explain to Kicker's mum.

Kicker was as red as a grey mouse can go with excitement. He was desperate to play. This was tricky. Even against the smallest seven-year-old human, Kicker hadn't got a hope, but he didn't seem to care.

"Kicker," yelled Boris, "don't tackle that boy!"

Kicker and the ball flew up
into the air and landed near the
goal. Kicker shook his head,
dazed, but got up straight away,
shouting, "To me! To me! On
the head!"

He got his wish. A small girl kicked the ball and it landed right on his head. He gave a little squeal and looked up to see the goalkeeper in a state of shock.

He was quite a big seven-year-old boy, but he clearly did not like mice. "Help!" he shouted, rooted to the spot.

The small girl took her chance. She kicked the ball again and it sailed past the goalie's feet into the goal.

Kicker was a hero. His head had set up a goal. Of course, no-one except the goalkeeper knew that, and *he* wasn't telling anyone. He could hardly speak.

Everyone congratulated the little girl, but Kicker knew it was him — at least, he sort of knew.

The blow on the head had made him quite giddy. He wobbled off the field with a silly grin on his face.

Boris ran over to him. "Kicker, are you all right?" He shook his cousin but he couldn't get any sense out of him.

"I scored. On the head . . . on *my* head," mumbled Kicker. He could hardly walk.

Boris thought they had better hide. The goalkeeper looked as if he might throw the ball at them too. Boris spotted an empty plastic bag under a tree and managed to get Kicker inside.

Hiding in the bag, Boris wondered how they would get home. He had no idea where they were.

# Chapter Four

After the children had gone
home the referee picked up the
ball. It was filthy. Then he
noticed an empty plastic bag
under a tree. He put the ball into
the bag, put the bag in his
rucksack and set off for the tube.

Boris and Kicker had the
football right on top of them.
They could hardly move but
Boris could still hear Kicker
congratulating himself: "On my
head!" he was saying. "I am the
champion."

"Good grief," said Boris. He
bit a small hole through the
plastic bag and
the rucksack to
see where they
were going. He
glimpsed the down escalator at
the tube station just as the
referee tripped over.

The plastic bag flew out of the rucksack and then bounced down every single step of the escalator. It was not a comfortable ride, even on a bouncy ball.

No-one noticed a scruffy old plastic bag bouncing around. It rolled on down a tunnel, kicked along in a crowd of people.

Boris was beginning

to feel rather unwell when the ball finally came to a halt. "I think we've stopped moving," he whispered. He made the hole a bit bigger and looked out.

"Oh no," he sighed. "Kicker, we're back on a train."

And indeed they were.

"Where are we going?" asked Kicker, finally paying attention to their troubles.

"I don't know. It could be anywhere. There are hundreds of tube stations."

Boris wondered if he would ever see his mum again. He very much wanted to cry, but he didn't because Kicker had started to.

When the train stopped at the next station Boris pushed his head out of the hole. He saw a man standing next to the bag, and then he did a very naughty thing. He reached out and gently bit the man on the ankle.

The man yelled and kicked
out, sending the plastic bag high
into the air. It was a big kick
and both the football and the
mice were ejected from the bag
like tiny space rockets.

## Chapter Five

Boris could hear the train set off again but he didn't seem to be on it. He lay on his back, checking that no bones were broken. He could hear Kicker – "Where . . . are . . . we?" he was sobbing, no longer the brave footballer.

Boris opened one eye and looked about. He and Kicker were surrounded by old crisp packets and sweet wrappers. "I think we're in a bin," he decided. He got up and looked over the edge. Below him, he could see the football.

LITTER

"Where . . . where . . . are we?" gulped Kicker.

"I don't know," said Boris. He peered out, fearing the worst. Then he saw the sign.

"CAMDEN TOWN" it said in huge letters above his head. Boris blinked and looked again. The sign definitely said "Camden Town". They were in the bin Heavy Duty used to collect rubbish!

"Kicker, Kicker, we're home!"
cried Boris. He helped his cousin
out of the bin and soon they
were dancing with excitement
on the platform.

Just then Heavy Duty
appeared with his broom. "Well,
I'll be—" he said. "There's that
football that Mrs Brett lost. Isn't
that wonderful? It's exactly
where she dropped it."

61

He picked up the ball and
walked off with it. "She *will* be
pleased."

Boris sighed with relief at
being home.

Suddenly he saw his mum
scurrying along with a bit of old
cream cracker for her children's
tea.

"Boris?" she said crossly. "Are you still here? This is where I left you this morning. Haven't you done anything all day?"

Boris looked at his cousin and smiled. "We've been playing football, haven't we, Kicker?" he said.

Kicker nodded, still feeling a little dazed.

"Have you been getting in Heavy Duty's way?" asked Boris's mum.

"Oh no, Mum," said Boris. "It was . . . um . . . . an away match."

Boris and Kicker grinned at each other and went home for tea.

THE END